DISNEY'S
Cinderella
The Perfect Dress

MOUSE
WORKS

Tonight there was to be a grand ball at the palace, and Cinderella didn't have a thing to wear! If only she could fix the hand-me-down dress she had found in the attic--but her stepmother had a million other things for her to do.

As Cinderella ironed her stepsisters' petticoats, shined their fancy patent leather shoes, and curled and brushed their hair, she imagined herself wearing a brand new elegant, floor-length gown.

Humming softly, Cinderella got lost in her daydream of elegant couples twirling around a breathtaking ballroom. What she didn't know was that Gus, Jaq, and their skillful animal friends were already hard at work, transforming Cinderella's plain hand-me-down dress.

Following a pattern in an old book, they sewed on big satin bows and long silk sashes, delicate ruffles and velvety ribbons. Then they snipped and tucked until they had created a gown fit for a princess.

When Cinderella opened the door to her tiny attic room she couldn't believe her eyes. "Oh, thank you! Thank you! It's beautiful!" she gasped as she quickly changed into the lovely dress and ran down the stairs. She had to catch her stepmother and stepsisters before they left without her!

But Cinderella looked so pretty in her new gown that her ugly stepsisters flew into a jealous rage. They began to tear the dress to shreds, claiming the beads and ribbons and sashes belonged to them.

As her stepmother and stepsisters rode off to the palace, Cinderella ran to the garden sobbing. Her hopes of going to the ball were dashed forever. When suddenly, a voice said, "Dry those tears." It was Cinderella's Fairy Godmother.

With a wave of her magic wand, the Fairy Godmother
created a shining coach, four beautiful white horses, a
driver, and a footman to whisk Cinderella off to the ball.
Everything glistened in the magical moonlight.

"But my dress..." Cinderella whispered, looking down at the
pitiful one she wore. In an instant, her Fairy Godmother adorned
her from head to toe in a dazzling gown and sparkling glass
slippers. Cinderella had never seen such an enchanting dress.
She felt like a princess.

That night, everyone agreed that Cinderella was by far the most beautiful woman at the ball--especially the Prince, who danced every dance with her alone.